Dressed in a furry hat and coat, little Herman looks just like a bear. And that's exactly what a bear who passes Herman in the woods thinks.

In fact, this bear thinks Herman is his own cousin Julius—and before the little boy can protest, the bear drags him off to his cave for an affectionate reunion with the rest of the bear family.

What a predicament for Herman! No matter what he does, the bears won't believe he's a boy. Herman sings, dances, and whistles – but the bears just applaud admiringly and decide he's the most talented bear in the family!

Finally, the bears get ready to hibernate for the winter, and Herman says comic tale. Herman's silly predicament is just the kind of humor young readers enjoy most. And the warm, lighthearted illustrations perfectly fit the mood of the text.

Bernice Myers is a well-known illustrator of children's books. *Not THIS Bear!* happily marks her debut as an author-artist.

Not THIS Bear!

Story and pictures by

BERNICE MYERS

FOUR WINDS PRESS
NEW YORK

Published by Four Winds Press
A Division of Scholastic Magazines, Inc.
New York, New York

Printed in the United States of America
Library of Congress Catalogue Card Number: 68-12388

For Marc and Danny

Little Herman
went to visit his
Aunt Gert.
He got off the bus at the
last stop.
But he still had
a short walk
to her house.

It was
very very
cold.

And to keep warm,
Herman pulled himself
deeper
inside his
long furry coat.

And he pulled
his big furry hat
down
down
over his face.

He looked just like
a bear—

which is funny,
because
that is exactly what
a passing bear
thought he looked like.

"You must be
my Cousin Julius!"
said the bear.

Grabbing Herman
by the hand,
the bear ran with him
to his cave.

“Look who I found
at the edge of the woods!” he shouted.

All the bears ran over
and kissed Herman
hard and wet.
"Cousin Julius, Cousin Julius!"
they shouted.

"My name is Herman,"
said Herman.
But no one even heard.
They were so excited.

"I'm not a bear...,"
Herman said.

"Dinner is ready,"
Mama Bear called.
"Take your places.
Cousin Julius,
you sit
here."

When Mama Bear
served the soup,
all the bears lapped it up
with their tongues.

But not Herman.
He ate politely
with a spoon
that he happened to have
in his pocket.

And when the vegetables
were served,
Herman ate with a fork
that he happened to have
in his pocket.

The bears were
amazed.
"My, my!" Big Brown Bear
stared at Herman.
"How smart
you are
to learn a trick
like that."

And all the bears
clapped,
as if they were watching
a circus act.

Poor Herman.
He wasn't a bear.
He was a little boy.

He was sure of it.
But the bears
were just as sure that Herman
was their Cousin Julius.

"So," thought Herman,
"I'll just prove
I'm really
a boy!"

He began to sing
and dance

and whistle;
tie his shoelace
and

stand on his
head—

—all the things a boy
knows how
to do.

But whatever he did,
the bears still thought
Herman
was a bear.
And they clapped even harder
at his tricks.

"See what happens," said Papa,
"when a bear has a chance
to go to the big city
and learn a trade."

“What a clever cousin
we have,” said Big Brown Bear.
And he yawned
and went outside.

Big Brown Bear
looked at the sky
and announced the time
of year – winter.

“After Mama’s big meal
we won’t have to eat again
until spring,” he said.
And all the bears
got ready
to sleep.

"Remember, we sleep
for at least
two months,"
said Big Brown Bear.

"Two months!" said Herman.
"I only sleep one night
at a time.
During the day I go out
and play.
I'm not sleeping through the winter!"

Z-Z-z-z-z-z

"But all bears do,"
said a baby bear.

"Not THIS bear," answered Herman.
"I like winter," he said.

"He likes winter," said the bears, astonished.

"Yes. I like winter.
I like to go sledding
and to skate.
I like to make
snow men and
drink hot cocoa with whipped cream.

"I like snowball fights
with my friends,
and I like to make
giant tracks
in the snow.

"And besides,
I have to go to school."

When Herman finished speaking,
there was a
long
silence.

Then Big Brown Bear
spoke.
"Perhaps you aren't a bear
after all.
In fact,
now that I look
closer,
you don't even have
a nose
like a bear."

"Look!" shouted a bear,
removing Herman's
furry hat and
coat.
"He's not a bear at all."

And

there,

shivering in the cave,

stood little Herman.

"See, I *am* a boy,"

he said.

Papa Bear
roared
with laughter.
"That's the best trick
of all.
And the trick
was on us."

Herman put on his
furry hat and coat again.
He said good-bye
to all
the bears.

"Come and visit us in spring,"
they yawned after him.

"I will," he answered,
just to be polite.

And Herman began to walk
toward Aunt Gert's house.

He was almost out
of the woods when
a big black burly
bear
jumped out from behind a tree.

Running toward Herman, the bear shouted,
"Cousin Bernard, Cousin Bernard..."

But Herman ran
just as fast as he could
out of the woods.

Herman was glad when he finally
reached
Aunt Gert's porch.

And Aunt Gert
was very glad
to see Herman.